For anyone who's ever taught a student like Zoey
or me. Thank you. —A.L.

HarperCollins

Chicken in School
Copyright © 2017 by HarperCollins Publishers
All rights reserved. Manufactured in China.
No part of this book may be used or reproduced in any manner whatsoever without written
permission except in the case of brief quotations embodied in critical articles and reviews.
For information address HarperCollins Children's Books, a division of HarperCollins
Publishers, 195 Broadway, New York, NY 10007.
www.harpercollinschildrens.com

Library of Congress Control Number: 2015015544
ISBN 978-0-06-236413-5

The artist used Adobe Photoshop to create the digital illustrations for this book.
Typography by Joe Merkel
17 18 19 20 21 SCP 10 9 8 7 6 5 4 3 2 1

❖

First Edition

CHICKEN in SCHOOL

By **Adam Lehrhaupt**

Illustrated by **Shahar Kober**

HARPER

An Imprint of HarperCollinsPublishers

Zoey wasn't like the other chickens.

And that's how Sam liked it.

"Where are the kids going?" asked Zoey.

"It's the first day of school," said Sam.

"I've always wanted to go to school. . . ."

"You have?" asked Zoey.

"Yes!" said Sam. "There are snacks at school."

But Zoey was already off.

She made a plan.

She went back for her pig.

"Put your thinking cap on, Sam," said Zoey. "We're going to school!"
"Hooray!" said Sam. "What's for snack?"

But Zoey was off again.

Clara almost spit out her cud.
"What's that chicken doing now?" she asked.

"We're going to school," said Sam.

"School?" said Clara. "You don't have a classroom. You can't have school if you don't have a classroom."

"I want to go to school," said Pip. "School has books."

"Me too!" said Henry. "I want to go to school. School has crayons."

"And snacks," said Sam. "Don't forget snacks."

DING! DING! DING!

"I made a school!" said Zoey.

"Well," said Clara. "Where's the teacher?"
"And where are the snacks?" asked Sam.

"I can be the teacher," said Zoey.
"First lesson: This is a book. Books
are for—"

"Building imagination!" said Zoey.

"Next lesson," said Zoey. "These are crayons. Crayons are for—"

"Coloring!" said Henry.

"Creating adventures!" said Zoey.

"Finally," said Zoey, "we skip math and go straight to recess."
Clara couldn't take any more.
"That's not right!" said Clara. "Books are for reading! Crayons are for coloring! And you can't skip math!"

"We skipped snack!" cried Sam.

"But recess is fun," said Zoey.

"Math is fun, too!" said Clara. "Watch!"

"If we have one pie and we add one more pie . . . how many pies will we have?"

"Two!" said Pip.

"Three," said Zoey. "Because
I found a pie for Sam."

"School is the BEST!" said Sam.

"Which part?"
asked Clara.

"The books?" asked Pip.

"The crayons?"
asked Henry.

"The snacks?" asked Zoey.

"Everything!" said Sam. "Because I was with you."

"If you thought that was fun," said
Zoey, "wait until you try recess."